Maple Fool's Day

A Newfound Lake Cozy Mystery
Book II

Virginia K. Bennett

To the members of the writing community who supported me early on, thank you!

Skye Jones
Marissa Farrar
Dawn Edwards
Kat Reads Romance
Kathryn LeBlanc
TL Swan
VR Tennent
Gina Sturino
Rachelle Kampen
...and so many more!

Table of Contents

Chapter 1

The Shack

APRIL FOOLS' DAY WAS ONE OF REBECCA'S TOP-three favorite holidays. When asked, she'd begrudgingly admit it wasn't a 'real' holiday, but she looked forward to it every year. Though she never would have dreamed of committing such an offense herself, she fondly remembered the day in seventh grade when a fellow classmate put chalk in the math teacher's coffee mug. That spark happened the year before classmates stuffed lengths of chalk in the erasers on the chalk tray at the front of the room for the new math teacher. Rebecca would never confess to being involved in any pranks, but still carried the guilt from that day when she let her friend, Abby, take the fall. From middle school on, people close to Rebecca knew to avoid her on April Fools' Day.

This year, April Fools' Day fell on the Monday after Easter, when the local library Rebecca oversaw was scheduled to be closed. Not to be deterred, Rebecca announced at the start of the new year she would be hosting gatherings on April first for the children around Newfound Lake, in honor of such an important day on the calendar.

Young children had the earliest time slot with their parents for read-alouds of silly picture books and color-changing art with Karen, the retired art teacher turned author. Slightly older kids, ones who were out of kindergarten after lunch, could listen to Rebecca read books where kids played pranks on each other but ultimately learned their lesson. Karen would also host an art project making straw-berries; they were made out of pink paper and straws as a prank to take home. The after-school crew, ones who walked to the library from the elementary or middle school, would be part of STEM projects that allowed them to pull pranks, safe ones, on their siblings and parents. Jeremy, a retired teacher, would volunteer in the afternoon so Rebecca wasn't left to fend for herself.

With Easter being early this year, before Rebecca could enjoy her favorite holiday, Melanie and Megan got to enjoy one of theirs. Kenny Towne, Rebecca's fiancé, attended the Easter church service in the morning with the girls and his ex-wife, Heather. Religion was important to Heather, so Kenny felt that continuing to support the girls' exploration of faith, at least for a little while longer, was prudent.

Things were complicated with the living arrangements of the three adults now sharing the responsibility of raising the girls, so they wanted to keep it as simple as possible until after Kenny and Rebecca were officially married. Being divorced meant that only one parent got to enjoy that magical time immediately after waking on a holiday. As a result, Kenny planned a special afternoon with the girls and Rebecca.

"Where are we going, Dad?" Megan asked her father in the parking lot of the church after Rebecca met them at his SUV.

"We're going to wait until we're all buckled in, and then I'll tell the three of you."

"Wait, Rebecca, you don't know where we're going?"

Rebecca let out a little chuckle. "Girls, I was told to dress warm and wear boots. That's all I know."

The girls loaded into their booster seats and found all of their warm winter gear in the back.

"Dad," the newly turned nine-year-old Melanie announced, "we are wearing our Easter dresses. How will we put on snow pants?"

"Let's go to my house because it's close, and we can figure out changing into your winter gear." Rebecca added, "I'll leave my car there so we can ride together. Sound good?"

"I brought a change of clothes for all of us, but I forgot to plan the changing part. Rebecca's house works perfectly."

Rebecca walked back to her car and drove to her house, followed by Kenny, Melanie and Megan. The adults carried the winter gear into the house and helped the girls, when needed, to change into pants and sweaters as well as the snow pants and boots. Rebecca's two cats were nowhere to be seen due to the volume of bodies and noise. When the family of four made their way back out to the SUV, the questions about the mystery trip started again.

"Can you tell us where we're going now, Dad?" asked Melanie, rolling her eyes more and more like a teenager every day.

"We're going to Hill to learn about how to make maple syrup."

Melanie chimed in. "We know how maple syrup is made. They brought someone to the elementary school to do a demonstration last year at an assembly."

"Yes, but did they take you to an old sugar shack in the woods?"

At just seven, Megan had her head cocked to the side as she asked. "Is it on a hill?"

"It is in Hill, the town," responded Kenny.

"Ohhhhh."

Hill was a small town south of Bristol, known to most because of Old Hill Village, which was razed and moved due to a flood control project in the forties, and the historic elementary school. Due to the name, Hill was often mistaken for a land feature instead of a town.

"If we're going to Hill, it's a good thing we're taking your vehicle," proclaimed Rebecca.

The weather today was chilly, but mostly because of the wind. The roads in many parts of Hill were dirt, and mud season was in full swing. Locals liked to say they had five seasons instead of four: Spring, Summer, Fall, Winter and Mud.

"I wouldn't have it any other way. From what I've

heard, we're practically facing a roller coaster to get to our destination."

Kenny drove from Rebecca's house near the center of Bristol, along 3A, and took a couple turns, passing over Smith River, where the road eventually turned to dirt. A roller coaster was an appropriate comparison, as the SUV traversed massive ruts that moved under the weight of the vehicle. After several minutes of feeling like they were on an amusement park ride, he pulled into a driveway on the left side of Borough Road.

"I can't say I'm upset for that to be over," reported Rebecca, wrapping her auburn hair in a messy bun then covering it with a winter hat.

Kenny turned off the engine. "Everyone, let's put on our coats, hats and gloves."

After about five minutes, the motley crew disembarked from all doors of the vehicle onto a squishy driveway.

"Once again, I'm glad we took your vehicle," said a smug Rebecca, looking at the state of his wheel wells and their boots.

He smiled at her in response. "Let's go." They headed in the direction of the old farmhouse.

A man in a once-beige-now-vintage Carhartt jacket came lumbering in their direction. "I'm over here," he called out. "Head this way." The man who seemed to be in his seventies waved for them to walk to their left. Though he was probably taller in his youth, his hunched posture put him around Rebecca's five-foot-six height.

"Joseph, thanks for having us over today." The initial

wave turned into a rugged handshake on the part of both men.

"Never a problem helping out our local law enforcement." The old man winked. Once again, it appeared to Rebecca that Kenny had used every available connection to make things happen for his daughters.

"We missed Maple Weekend at the bigger operations due to an active investigation, but I'm excited that we did. I've been looking forward to this all week." His enthusiasm made Rebecca feel warm inside. It was Kenny's actions that made the girls feel loved, not just words. "This is my fiancé, Rebecca Ramsey. She's the librarian in Bristol. And these are my daughters, Melanie and Megan." He gestured to each in turn. "Girls, this is Mr. Josephson."

"Maple Weekend isn't something we participate in, so getting to show you all how we make syrup is a rare treat." He beamed with pride.

Melanie spoke up. "Your name is Joseph Josephson?"

"That's right. I was the eighth of nine boys. I think my parents ran out of names before they got to me." Everyone laughed.

"Well, what can you show us today, Mr. Josephson?"

"Call me Joe, Kenny. No need to be formal around here."

"Joe, where do we start?"

Mr. Josephson took the group out into the woods, behind the farmhouse, where he showed them the buckets he used to collect sap and the taps that had been inserted into the tree that allowed sap to flow out. "They are telling us to stop using these old metal ones because they're not food-grade something or other, but I'm too old to change my ways and invest a bunch of money in a hobby." He pulled a rusty red Radio Flyer wagon behind him with large containers inside. Kenny offered to pull it and was denied.

"I'm pretty sure we'll all survive," joked Kenny. "I drank my fair share of water from a hose when I was a kid, and look at me now." He held his arms out, showing his trim figure and the shampoo-commercial hair style that hadn't changed since high school waving with the breeze.

"I even had someone come by trying to buy them off me to turn them into lamps, if you can believe it. At this point, I've got more trees than I do buckets, so I can't afford to go sell any."

"Not having your sap buckets sure would leave you in a sticky situation." It took a moment, but the girls laughed at Rebecca's joke eventually.

Once they had collected sap from several trees and deposited it in the portable containers, Mr. Josephson pulled the wagon back, even slower this time, to the front of his property. "We're taking these to the sugar shack," he told the girls, pointing at the mini log cabin with smoke billowing from the stone chimney. "Same shack my parents built when I was a kid. Before then, my grandparents used an open fire between the back side of the farmhouse and the woods. I was born in that house." He pointed at the farmhouse in front of Kenny's SUV. "I was the only kid who hadn't moved away after graduation, so it was left to me when my father passed away. I got this sugar shack in the process." They entered the shabby structure with a warning not to touch anything metal once inside.

Down the center of the cabin was a three-by-six-foot metal pan three-quarters full of sap with space on either side for someone to walk around and not much else. Below the pan was the wood stove, fully enclosed, with doors on either side for adding wood. There was one stool at the far end, but that was maybe only ten feet from the door they entered. With no windows, the space was illuminated by a propane lantern.

After each member of the group added the sap they had collected to the pan, Rebecca asked, "Mr. Josephson, how many gallons of sap does it take to make maple syrup?"

He paused to wipe his brow with a red handkerchief from an inside breast pocket. "This year, it seems we're averaging about forty, but some years it's been more or less."

"Forty gallons of sap, the stuff we collected from the trees, to make one gallon of the syrup we put on our pancakes?" questioned Melanie, shock evident in her eyes and voice.

"I thought you already knew everything from that talk at school." Her father looked at her over the steam that had begun to hover above the sap in the metal pan. Below the pan was a fire Mr. Josephson must have started before they had arrived.

"Maybe I wasn't listening to *everything*," she admitted.

"Well, this system is designed to make enough syrup for a family, with the occasional gift handed out." Mr. Josephson winked, this time at Melanie.

Over the course of the next hour, they talked about the specifics, both inside and outside the shack, when it came to the intensity of the fire under the evaporation pan, the temperature at which sap boils, the amount of wood needed for the season, the operation of the chimney and how to bottle the finished product.

"Yesterday, I made some syrup and poured a couple bottles for you to take home."

Rebecca protested. "Mr. Josephson, you don't need to do that. Keep it for yourself."

"Ms. Ramsey, I'm happy to teach the next generation the old way of doing things and pass along the fruits of my labor. They should get something for helping today, anyway."

Kenny prompted, "Girls, what do you say?"

"Thank you," they sang in unison, hugging their bottles of liquid sweetness.

"You are very welcome. Just remember how much sap and time it takes to make it when you're eating some." They nodded vigorously.

After everyone had exited the sugar shack, Rebecca and Kenny both shook hands with Mr. Josephson.

"We really appreciate you doing this for the girls, and for us. Maybe some day I could come and take more lessons in case I want to continue the old ways on my own property, if you have the time." Kenny looked hopeful.

"Time's running out this season, but I'd be happy to next year when we start the process so you can follow through from start to finish. It's not something you learn in a few hours. Lots of variables Mother Nature still has control over."

"Understood. Well, thanks for taking it into consideration." Kenny walked back to his SUV with Rebecca at his side.

"Is that a hobby you're really interested in?" she asked.

"I think I could enjoy it, why?"

"We'd have to live somewhere that had plenty of maple trees on the property for that to happen."

"I guess we would. That is a great topic to include when you finally agree to talk about living arrangements once we're married." He pecked her cheek before opening the passenger's door and closing it behind her once inside. He checked that both girls had their jackets off and had buckled securely before closing each of their doors as well. The drive back down Borough Road was just as adventurous as the way up had been, and all passengers were happy when they transitioned to pavement.

When they returned to Rebecca's house, they entered with the intention of eating an early Easter supper so Kenny could get the girls in their beds at a reasonable time for a Sunday evening. She had prepared a crockpot ham that morning, so all she needed to do was turn on the burners to cook vegetables and warm up some rolls in the oven.

"You know you didn't have to go through all this trouble for us," Kenny said as the girls finished getting their gear off.

"It's Easter. Of course there had to be an Easter supper. What would you have cooked?"

Kenny sheepishly looked at the floor. "I would have gone back to Heather's with them to eat dinner that she cooked." He quickly stood up for himself. "I can manage regular meals, but a full supper like this is beyond my planning capabilities."

Rebecca moved seamlessly about the kitchen while the girls made pudding slime at the table like they had a couple weeks ago with her. This time, they did the measuring themselves with the provided supplies on the table. When she was about five minutes away from serving dinner, Kenny helped the girls pick up and replace their mess with plates and utensils.

The table was full of side dishes worth drooling over. She had a simple dish of asparagus with butter and lemon, a dish of steamed green beans for the girls, a plate of deviled eggs she had stored in the fridge from earlier in the morning, a bowl of whipped potatoes, a large maple-glazed ham with pineapple chunks, rolls, and a dish of raisin sauce.

"How did you? Where did you?" Kenny tripped over his words.

Rebecca had secured the recipe for the raisin sauce his grandmother always made with Easter supper. She had passed away many years ago, but his mother had her box of recipe cards. "After the number of times you told me about this raisin sauce, how could I not make it?" Rebecca's actions also spoke louder than words when it came to showing her love for others as well.

They enjoyed Easter supper at her large table, wondering how many might join them at it in the future. Thanksgiving had been a success overall, if you ignore the minor interruption, but Easter fell on the night before a school day. In the future, if it fell before a school break like it had the previous year, Rebecca was open to making it a much larger family event, especially as the girls got older.

When it was time to leave, Kenny said, "I'll bring the girls after school to the STEM activity, if there is still space."

"I already signed them up," she replied then turned her focus to Melanie and Megan. "Have a great day at school tomorrow, and don't pull any pranks I wouldn't pull." She showed them crossed fingers when she spoke then waved goodbye as the trio headed to the SUV, arms laden with snowpants, hats and gloves. She overheard Kenny's response, telling them not to pull *any* pranks at school tomorrow.

Exhausted, Rebecca entered her quiet house and appreciated the less demanding lovebugs that finally appeared when she closed the door behind her.

Chapter 2

The Prank

Rebecca flopped onto the couch and was immediately visited by both of her feline housemates. Bean and Joey were rubbing on her elbows and curling up on her lap, vying for her attention.

"I'm sorry it was hectic when I got home." She nuzzled under Bean's chin and stroked the black fur along Joey's back. "It's just me for the rest of the night." She sat with them for a long time, appreciating the slow rise and fall of their bodies as they napped on and near her. When she finally needed to get up to use the bathroom and get ready for bed, they stayed on the couch.

This was an early night for Rebecca. Before turning in, she sent a text to Kenny.

Rebecca: See you tomorrow afternoon at the library.

Rebecca: Love you! XOXO

She laid out a shirt for the following day that read 'I Don't Trust Anyone Today,' a colorful jester standing out against the black t-shirt. She paired it with a green zip-up hoodie and straight-leg jeans cuffed at the bottom. She realized, once her evening routine was done, she had forgotten to pack a lunch. Knowing there wouldn't be time to breathe tomorrow, bringing something was important.

Her legs felt heavy as she made her way back downstairs, careful not to be too loud as she walked through the living room. She made a quick salad that included leftover ham from dinner but none of the raisin sauce. Satisfied she was in good shape for April Fools' Day, she returned to her bedroom to watch a show called The Cleaner on BritBox. Rebecca couldn't help but think there must be someone locally who had to do this job after she discovered a body and the police were done with the crime scene. All at once, she both hoped she'd meet them and never need to meet them at the same time.

It was strange to wake up to a murder scene on her television, but that's what she got for falling asleep during a show about a man who was responsible for cleaning up the aftermath. The getting ready process was quick after turning off the television. She wanted to be in the library bright and early to help Karen get ready for the youngest visitors.

The library always felt like it was just waking up when Rebecca keyed in and turned the lights on. Typically, it got to sleep on Sunday and Monday, but April Fool's Day was an exception. She had spent all week choosing the books she would read and had already practiced reading them out loud. Karen got there shortly after Rebecca, massive totes in hand.

"Let me help you." Rebecca hit the button for the automatic doors and relieved Karen of the clear, plastic boxes she was already wrestling with. "How many more are there?"

"Four, I think." Karen returned to her vehicle while Rebecca brought the first two into the multi-purpose room at the far end of the building. She crossed paths with Karen as she carried the next two. Pressing the button again to open the doors, Rebecca grabbed the remaining totes from Karen's vehicle and walked in with them.

"I think this is it," Rebecca announced. Karen went outside, allowing the doors to close, and moved her car to a parking space instead of blocking the entrance. When she returned, she was all business.

"Do you have time to help me set up?" she asked Rebecca.

"I'm all yours. I really appreciate you coming in today to humor me."

"Does that mean I am immune to your pranks?" Karen stopped, waiting for the answer.

Rebecca sighed. "I guess. I'll just save them up for Jeremy."

The day passed by in a blur. Karen had set up an activity for the smallest patrons to mix paint colors with their hands for after Rebecca's read-aloud. They put one hand in yellow paint and made a handprint on a piece of posterboard, with the help of the parent attending. Second, they placed their other hand in red paint and made a handprint. Finally, they mixed the paint together, getting their hands all messy, and placed two handprints under the first two in orange. The activity was repeated two more times to make green and purple handprints from the provided primary colors.

The second group also had two books followed by an activity that took a lot more prep work. Karen had cut out pink strawberries from construction paper and sliced lines through them. There was also a huge bucket of straw pieces of varying sizes. She taught the children, and adults, how to weave the straws through the slits to create straw-berries. Once complete they got to add a green stem to the top. The joke was to bring the hidden strawberry home and offer it to someone who would otherwise assume they were going to receive a real piece of fruit then pull it out from behind the back saying, "April Fools!"

During what should have been Rebecca's lunch, she helped Karen clean and pack up. The library was only open for the scheduled activities, so she didn't need to worry about regular patrons showing up. Jeremy, however, let himself into the library around one to get ready for the afternoon session.

Rebecca walked out of the multi-purpose room to greet Jeremy with a huge bucket in her arms. Looking at her struggling with the bucket, Jeremy offered to carry it for her.

"That's okay. It's just the water we used to clean the paint brushes with. I'm heading outside to dump it." As soon as she finished speaking, and right in front of Jeremy, she tripped, launching the bucket in his direction.

Jeremy's face contorted, attempting to both turn away from the impending water to the face, and hoping he might be able to somehow catch the bucket and prevent the disaster from happening. When he grabbed the bucket in mid-air, confetti splashed him in the face.

"Gotcha. April Fools!" Rebecca slapped her knee and laughed.

Brushing off the confetti onto the floor of the library, Jeremy responded, "You sure did. Now, the joke's on you. You'll need to vacuum it while I get ready." He sauntered past Rebecca.

In the same multi-purpose room, Jeremy was preparing to entertain kids from age seven through as old as twelve. Rebecca, after she finished vacuuming, inhaled her salad then checked on Jeremy.

"Are we all set. Kids are expected soon."

He took another look around the room. "Pretty sure we're good. I've set up stations that you and I will rotate through with directions at each. We'll start at these two first then both swap to the other two." He pointed in turn.

"You gave me the easy ones, right?"

"They're all easy, Rebecca."

The kids who had signed up were divided into two groups. Rebecca put Melanie and Megan in different groups even though Megan was a bit older than the rest of the kids in hers. She wanted them to have independent experiences whenever possible. Things were so busy, she didn't get to say two words to Kenny as he dropped the girls off, though she did catch Jeremy reminding him when pick-up was.

Rebecca managed to make it through running her two activities, both based on disposable cups. First, the kids made a mixture that imitated hot chocolate, but it solidified to a high shine. They put the mixture in a tipped over paper cup so it looked like the hot chocolate had spilled all over the table. This was first, so the mixture had time to firm up before they went home. The second was less science and more fun. They wrote on post-it notes that there was a dangerous spider under the cup then used their fingers to poke and rip a hole into the side of the cup, making it look like the spider had escaped. The best part was listening to the kids brag about who they would play the pranks on and how well they predicted the gags would work.

When all was said and done, the day was a huge success. Kenny came to pick up the girls, but there was so much to clean, she just waved as Jeremy checked them out and got a signature for the two participants.

For well over thirty minutes, Rebecca and Jeremy were making trips back and forth to the bathroom sink to clean things up and out to his vehicle to drop off supplies to go home with him. At one point, Rebecca noticed that Jeremy hadn't returned for several minutes. Worried that something was wrong, she went out to the parking lot.

"Jeremy." She waited. It was still light out, so that was good, but she didn't see him anywhere. "Jeremy?" After no response, she walked over to his car. He had backed into his parking space, so the driver's side door was on the opposite side of the vehicle, but she could see that it was wide open. Her car was on the far side of his. "That's weird," she said to herself. When she got to his door, she found Jeremy lying on the ground, arms and legs spread, face to the side.

"Jeremy!" she yelled. Since the door would hit him is she closed it, she ran around the car to get to him from the rear of the vehicle. She fell to the ground on her knees, placing her fingers against his neck. When she did this, she immediately felt a strong pulse.

"April Fools!" he said, turning his head more to look over his shoulder at her.

She brought her arm back and swung with all the power she possessed and then some, connecting with his shoulder. "Jeremy Allen Shelton, how could you do that to me? I thought you were dead. That's the absolute worst... I can't even." Still on her knees, she sat back on her feet and started to cry.

"Awww, Rebecca. I thought you loved April Fools' Day. I figured you'd get a kick out of this." He quickly sat up and gave her a hug.

"Tomorrow I'll appreciate how well you pulled this off, but today, today I'm really mad at you for making me think something bad had happened."

"Don't worry, I'm the worst that could possibly happen to you today."

They left the parking lot and wrapped up what was left in the library. Rebecca wiped the dried mud off the knees of her jeans while Jeremy was covered from head to toe in dried mud.

"Was it worth it?" she asked him, looking him up and down.

"Every second. I got you good! The queen has been dethroned."

"Until next year." It was both a threat and a promise. "You better sleep with one eye open, Jeremy." With that, the pair got into their respective cars and pulled out of the parking lot.

Rebecca had decided yesterday she wanted to pay Mr. Josephson for the maple syrup he gave them. She knew how much that product was worth and how much labor went into making it, so she wouldn't just let him give it away like that.

The temperature had dropped last night, so she gambled that making it up to his property on Borough Road would be possible with her Subaru. Thankfully, the trip had been uneventful, and she pulled in with no problem. She was surprised to see, however, that there was no smoke coming from the chimney of the small sugar shack.

Stepping out onto the hard driveway, she made her way over to the structure, noting that the door was fully closed and latched from the outside. When she knocked, there was no answer. Not wanting to trespass, she walked back toward the farmhouse and knocked on the front door. The woman who answered was unfamiliar.

"Who's there?" asked the woman still behind a pane of glass and a closed door.

"My name is Rebecca Ramsey. I was here yesterday

for a tour of Joseph's maple syrup setup. The police chief and I brought his two daughters."

"Then I'd go check the sugar shack for Joseph. He's not in here."

Rebecca found that odd. "I just checked there, and no one answered."

The woman opened the door wearing her bathrobe and slippers and gestured in the direction of the small cabin. "Just go open the door. I'm sure he's working on his syrup."

"Okay. Thank you, Mrs. Josephson." She made a mental note that she hadn't told Rebecca to use her first name.

Rebecca walked back over to the shack and rotated a large horizontally oriented piece of wood two hundred seventy degrees counterclockwise that had been holding the door shut behind a latch. When she pulled the door toward her, a huge plume of smoke escaped, knocking her back. As the smoke cleared, she could make out Mr. Josephson, slumped on the floor, unmoving, his hand holding a handkerchief near his face.

Chapter 3

The Veracity

Rebecca scrambled to get to his side, momentarily deterred by the large pan of dark brown sludge taking up far too much space in the small structure. The door closed behind her, leaving her in the dark, so she went back out to prop the door open. Returning to Mr. Josephson, she bent over his body and found what she thought was a weak pulse. Pulling her cell phone out of her back pocket after standing, she realized she had no service.

The woman who had been at the front door was no longer there, having returned to the farmhouse after pointing Rebecca in the direction of the sugar shack. The run to the front door seemed much further than the walk just moments ago in the opposite direction. Banging on the door brought her back after what felt like an hour.

"What do you need now?" asked the woman after opening the front door.

"Mr. Josephson is in there on the ground. I think he

might still have a pulse. We need to call an ambulance immediately!"

The woman didn't move. "So call one," she directed.

Rebecca was stunned. "I can't. If you aren't going to call, can I come in to make the call?" She was moments away from shoving the woman out of the way and locating the phone herself.

The woman Rebecca had assumed was Mrs. Josephson slowly backed out of the way. "Phone's on the wall in the kitchen." There was no gesture for what direction to go to get to the kitchen, but Rebecca wasn't going to wait.

As it turned out, the kitchen was directly ahead of her as she scanned the first floor. On the wall to her left, Rebecca found an avocado green phone hanging on the wall with a rotary dial, the cord twisted and bent in all directions. She lifted the receiver and listened as the nine ticks signified the first digit of the 9-1-1 call, then two separate, single ticks.

"9-1-1, what's your emergency?" came a male voice.

"I'm out on Borough Road in Hill." She turned to look at the woman standing just inside the front door. "What's the house number?" Rebecca asked with urgency.

"One sixty-three."

"One sixty-three, Borough Road, Hill. I have a male in his seventies who looks dead but might still have a pulse. You'll need to send an ambulance immediately."

"Can you check..."

"No, I can't. He's in the sugar shack outside, and I'm

attached to a wall rotary phone in the farmhouse. Please, just be quick."

"We already have someone on their way now. Any other information you can give us?"

"There was a lot of smoke when I opened the door, so I'm guessing smoke inhalation."

"Good to know."

"I'm going back outside to see if he is responsive. I'll hang up now. There is a green Subaru in the driveway." She hung up and blew past the woman who still hadn't moved even after hearing that Mr. Josephson might be dead.

Rebecca returned to the shack following the same path as before, noting that there were a lot of footprints around the area, not just hers. She had been there just over twenty-four hours before and didn't remember this many tracks, but had she really been paying attention?

The sirens took about four minutes to be heard and another minute before she saw an ambulance. She was thankful that the road had firmed up since yesterday, otherwise the ambulance might not have made it this far. When it pulled in, the sirens stopped.

She moved out of the shack where she had been waiting with Mr. Josephson since returning. There wasn't really anything she could do, so she had talked to him and shook him gently on his arm, hoping he would just open his eyes and wake up.

"Ma'am, we've got this," said the first EMT. A second entered the shack then exited when he realized there was nowhere for him. He went to retrieve some kind of board to transport the man since moving the ambulance any closer seemed either impossible or a waste of time.

The pair were able to maneuver Mr. Josephson out onto the board just as police cars were arriving. She was surprised to see Jacob, one of the officers who worked under Kenny, get out.

"Rebecca, what happened?"

"I came to pay Mr. Josephson for the maple syrup we got yesterday, but he was in there slumped on the floor. I think he had a pulse, but I'm not sure."

Jacob offered assistance to the EMTs who were loading the still unmoving body of Mr. Josephson into the back of the ambulance but was turned down. With the police car out of the way, the ambulance pulled out, turned the siren back on, and drove down the road toward civilization.

"Let's start at the beginning," Jacob said. Rebecca noted a second officer approaching the front door of the farmhouse.

"Jacob, I don't want to interrupt you, but you'll want to be over there to get a statement from her. She was acting strangely during this whole situation." He nodded. "Don't leave."

Jacob walked to the front door of the farmhouse with Rebecca hot on his heels. When he stopped quickly, she bumped into his back.

"I know I shouldn't have to tell you this, but don't say anything."

"My lips are sealed." She motioned to zip her lips.

Jacob stood next to a female officer, one Rebecca didn't recognize, who was asking questions.

"Ma'am, do you know what happened to the man the ambulance just removed."

"I'm going to assume it was my husband. Maybe he had too much to drink last night. I don't know." Her casual tone made Rebecca think maybe she hadn't heard the phone call to 9-1-1.

"When was the last time you saw your husband?"

She looked up then back at the officers on her doorstep. "Sometime yesterday."

"Is that unusual to go that long without seeing your husband?"

"Nah. This time of year, he practically lives in that shack. When he does come in, he sleeps in the first-floor bedroom because he smells so bad. The process is so all-consuming, he'll be right back out there before I wake up. You know how some women are football widows and others are baseball widows... I'm a maple syrup widow." It was clear to Rebecca that Mrs. Josephson didn't really register the gravity of what she had said.

"If you don't mind my saying, you don't seem very concerned that your husband was just taken by the ambulance."

Rebecca waited to hear this response because she had felt the same since she had arrived.

"He's an old Yankee. He's like a cat with nine lives. He's gonna be fine."

If the woman was only holding a lit cigarette,

Rebecca thought, it would have looked like a scene from a television show. She wished someone would yell, "Cut!"

The female officer asked, "Well, can you think of anyone who was here in the last twenty-four hours?"

"Joseph had people in and out of here all season. I do remember this lady." She pointed at Rebecca.

The female officer turned in Rebecca's direction showing her last name to be Adams. "We'll speak to her in a moment. Anyone else?"

"I think I saw Nelson and Warren pop by, and maybe Bobby's truck was here at some point." Officer Adams took out a notepad and started to write down names.

Jacob turned to walk away from the front door and into the driveway. Rebecca followed and noticed Kenny's SUV pulling in. They met close to the road as Kenny exited the driver's side.

"What do we know so far?" Kenny asked Jacob.

"Actually, I need to ask the two of you some questions first."

"Jacob, what are you doing?" Kenny looked at Rebecca's face then back to Jacob's.

Jacob straightened up as tall and official as he could. "You were here yesterday, correct?"

"Yes. Rebecca and I came with the girls to learn how to make maple syrup the old-school way. Didn't she already tell you that?"

"When you left, how was Mr. Josephson?"

"He was alive, if that's what you are asking. Why do I feel like I'm a suspect?"

Jacob continued. "And what time would you say you left the property yesterday?"

Kenny let out a big sigh. "What do you think, Rebecca, two? Two-thirty?"

"Sounds about right."

This time it was Jacob who inhaled deeply and let out the breath quickly. "Where was Mr. Josephson when you left?"

"Still in the sugar shack, at least I think he was."

Rebecca interjected, "I left with the girls and started to get them in the SUV, and Kenny said goodbye last. I wasn't really paying attention to them because I was focused on the girls."

Jacob turned to face Rebecca fully. "When you got here today, what did you see first?"

"I checked the sugar shack by knocking, but no one answered, so I went to the farmhouse. Mrs. Josephson answered and said to check for him in the shack again because he wasn't in the house. I opened the door and..." She closed her eyes with the memory. "So much smoke came out, it backed me up, practically took my breath away. I saw him on the floor when the smoke cleared, and I checked for a pulse. I'm not sure. I wanted there to be a pulse so badly, I could have imagined it, but I knew I had to call the ambulance."

"Do you have service out here?" Kenny pulled out his cell phone and looked at his screen. "I've got nothing."

"No. I ran to the farmhouse and practically had to force myself inside to call 9-1-1. She was just so unaffected. I told the operator what I just told you but in fewer words. As far as I know, Mrs. Josephson heard all of it and just stood there. I was able to finish the call and get back outside without her moving a muscle."

Kenny and Jacob both nodded but said nothing.

"Last question, Chief. Did you close the door behind you when you left the shack?"

"Tell me you are kidding."

"You're the one who trained me. Do you think I'm kidding?"

Kenny's shoulders dropped a couple inches. "No, and you're doing a great job. Thank you for being thorough. I don't think I closed the door. I feel like I let go of it, maybe letting it close on its own."

"Thanks. Rebecca, I know I'm going to have more questions for you later, but can you tell me what you touched?"

"Between today and yesterday, I touched parts of the inside all over and probably all over the door from entering and exiting several times."

"I noticed it's currently propped open. Do you know how it got that way?"

"I did that today when I got here after I saw him the first time because there wasn't any light inside."

"Noted."

Jacob asked a few more questions and left to talk to Officer Adams.

Once out of earshot, Kenny asked Rebecca, "What are you doing here, anyway?"

"I finished the library events and wanted to come pay

Mr. Josephson for the maple syrup he gave the girls. I know real maple syrup isn't cheap."

"That was kind of you. How are you doing?"

She needed to pause to consider how she really was feeling. "After Jeremy pretended to be dead in the parking lot then finding Mr. Josephson, I'm a bit on edge. Maybe I should have you check my house before I enter just to make sure everything is as it should be." She laughed, but it was an empty sound.

"I'll be here for a while, so why don't you head home. Do you think you can drive? Do you need someone to check the house?" The concern was evident in the wobble of his voice and how he bent down to make sure he was in her line of sight.

"I'll be fine to drive. That other thing was just a joke."

"I'm guessing Jacob will be the one to contact you if he needs more information, so probably nothing else tonight. Are you sure you're okay to drive?"

"Absolutely. I'm guessing I'll head to bed quickly. It's been a long day."

"Text me if you need anything. Love you." They didn't kiss because Chief Towne was on duty, and now Rebecca needed to start thinking about what would come next.

Chapter 4

The Family

REBECCA DROVE HOME, SHAKEN BY WHAT SHE HAD discovered. Mr. Josephson had been so kind to them just yesterday, and today he was on his way to the hospital, hopefully still fighting for his life. When she got home, she spent some time processing with her cats, after feeding them of course. The loveseat was a good size for the three of them to cuddle.

"I can't help but think that this wasn't an accident. I'm sure that this kind of thing could have been due to lack of sleep or maybe his age was a contributing factor, but he seemed fine yesterday." Joey and Bean weren't participating in the conversation, but they were great listeners. "Something just seems off, but I can't put my finger on it."

Rebecca thought about approaching the shack and needing to go to the farmhouse, assuming he wasn't still working on the maple syrup. The wife's nonchalant reaction to not knowing where he was set Rebecca's internal bells ringing.

"She just didn't seem concerned, which makes sense if he has a history of sleeping downstairs and going to check on the process at all hours of the night, but when I returned to use the phone, nothing changed." Rebecca must have changed the speed or pressure on the way she was petting Joey because he turned to look at her with slitted eyes. "Sorry."

When she replayed the scene of finding Mr. Josephson in her mind, she closed her eyes. She knocked on the door. Why had she knocked on the door? The door was closed. When she didn't get an answer, she turned the large handle; two hundred seventy degrees was what she told Jacob. Why did that matter? She imagined putting her hand on the piece of wood when it was horizontal, the end with a small nob pointing to the right. It sat behind a small vertical piece of wood keeping it in place, preventing the door from opening. The nob in her hand went up and to the left for the first ninety degrees, then down until it was pointed at the ground.

"I've got it," she shouted, startling the cats, causing them to jump down from their position on the loveseat with Rebecca. They stood on the floor of the living room, staring up at her. "The door opened out, right?" No response. "Well, that means the hinges are on the outside. He couldn't remove the hinge pins when he figured out he was trapped." The cats blinked. Bean started to lick at one paw. "And why was he trapped, you might ask?" They hadn't asked. "The lock couldn't have *happened* to fall shut. It had to be lifted up and over in order to lock him in." Rebecca looked at the cats, arms open and palms up, waiting for applause or at least some kind of recognition.

She ran upstairs and grabbed her laptop, unplugging it from the charger before running back downstairs with it. Now that it was clearly some kind of attack on Mr. Josephson, she needed to think about the who and the why.

As the computer booted up, she thought about the names Mrs. Josephson had rattled off to Officer Adams. "Oh, was it Nathan?" She rubbed her eyes with the heels of her hands, hoping she could recall the names. Realizing that this probably wasn't helping, she decided to start by looking up Joseph Josephson and go from there.

When she typed his name into the search bar, there were thousands of articles, but they were geographically all over the place. Since that wasn't going to work, she added Hill, New Hampshire to the search. One article popped up from the local newspaper, so she clicked on the link. What she found was an article about Joseph's family and how they had one of the oldest family-run farms in the area.

'Mr. Josephson tends to the cows, chickens and pigs while his wife is responsible for the vegetable garden. They grow their own corn for feed and can enough fruits and vegetables to last until the next growing season.'

Rebecca checked the date on the article and realized the Mr. Josephson named was actually Joseph's father. It continued to mention that they had nine children who all had responsibilities on the farm as well.

'Joseph is responsible for feeding the chickens and collecting eggs. When winter comes to an end, he works in the sugar shack with his father, making maple syrup for the family to eat all year round.'

Rebecca continued to read the article and noted that one of the other named children was Nelson. "That's it, Nelson. Mr. Josephson has a brother named Nelson who must have stopped over after we left yesterday." The cats had taken up spots on the floor more permanently, possibly assuming this was safer than trying to manage her outbursts. The article mentioned that Nelson was the oldest of the children. His responsibilities had been caring for the livestock and monitoring the next three children in line. With nine children, there had to be some babysitting done by the eldest siblings.

She opened a new tab and searched for Nelson Josephson in New Hampshire. She found that he had owned a restaurant in Franklin, the next town over, for over thirty years but was retired now.

"I guess he just stopped by to visit. It certainly didn't seem like Mrs. Josephson was fond of Nelson based on the way she lumped his name in with the others. When she continued to search, the names of his other siblings didn't sound familiar. She went back to searching for Nelson, and it turned out he now lived in Bristol and was a Rotarian. "Well, that's convenient," she said to herself, having given up talking to the cats. "I guess I'll try to see if I can track him down to have a little chat."

Figuring out the first name Mrs. Josephson had said triggered the rest of the list. Rebecca recalled Nelson, Warren and Bobby as the ones Officer Adams wrote down. The problem with searching for the name Warren was the town just over thirty minutes away with the same name. When she attempted it, she immediately saw the flaw. She tried several arrangements of words, but only came up with articles about the geographical location.

Rebecca found that searching for the name Bobby was even less helpful. Was Bobby short for Robert or the person's given name? No matter which was the answer, Bobby was an extremely popular name. The internet was often a helpful tool, but in this case, it seemed like boots on the ground and good questioning would be the answers.

Not wanting to waste time on more searches that would reveal zero leads, Rebecca headed into the kitchen. It wasn't too late to eat, but she also wasn't really hungry. She decided to make something for her lunch since the library was open the next day. However, she realized in time that her internal clock was off. The library had been open today, a Monday, though it typically wasn't. Tuesday, they opened late, and she'd have plenty of time in the morning to make something.

Her bedtime routine was brief and efficient. She was up the stairs and into the bed in about five minutes, with brushing her teeth being the largest time consumer. Her bed and pillows felt exceptionally good after such an emotional day. Before she drifted off to sleep, she tried to focus on how much fun the kids had for April Fools' Day but ended up dreaming about finding Jeremy in the parking lot.

When she woke for the final time, it was around seven. She had also woken at eleven, one, three and five to the image of Jeremy lying on the wet pavement. Each time, it took a few minutes to recall him getting up and joking about how he thought it would be funny. Rebecca wouldn't soon forget about his prank. She now had a full year to plan her revenge.

Her head was clear after getting up with the intention of making herself a breakfast of French toast with a small bottle of maple syrup she had from Mr. Josephson. Though he had gifted bottles to the girls, Kenny had managed an extra for Rebecca to take to her house.

She soaked two thick slices of bread for about thirty seconds in an egg batter that included vanilla and cinnamon, flipping it after fifteen. The skillet was already warm when she dropped in a tablespoon of butter, moving it around with a fork so the bread would be sure to land only on buttered areas. It took a few minutes on each side to fully cook. The plate needed a little color, so she washed some strawberries and cut them up to eat with the French toast. When the plate was full, she added the maple syrup.

The island in her kitchen was lonely with just her sitting at it. She missed having Kenny there when he had the girls. It was apparent the discussion about living arrangements needed to get moved up, especially with Sunday's mention of learning how to make maple syrup. Even if moving didn't happen until after they were married, having something to look forward to would help on the lonely days.

Rebecca sopped up sweet bites of bread and berries until only one final bite remained on her fork. Throughout her whole breakfast, thoughts of meeting Nelson swirled in her head. As she enjoyed the last of the delicious flavors, she thought about the sign she drove by every day on the way to the library. Apparently, she had driven by it so many times, she couldn't remember the specifics.

She got ready in a hurry, regardless of the fact her workday wouldn't start for several hours. Her phone had no messages, text or voice, though she thought maybe Kenny would send something personal to check on her. The April Fool's shirt of yesterday was now in the hamper, and Easter was in the rearview mirror, so she went with a neutral library t-shirt featuring the phrase 'Bookmarks are for quitters.' She so wanted to wear capris but wasn't sure about the weather holding out for the whole day; the way her life was going, she needed to be prepared. The beige shirt with pastel lettering was paired with stone-washed jeans and a pair of low-cut Converse. On her way out the door, she grabbed a charcoal-gray zip-up hoodie.

Her Subaru had some dirt caked in the wheel wells and splashed along the lower part of the doors, but her vehicle was much better off than Kenny's SUV had been on Easter after traversing the muddy Borough Road. She drove toward town without a final destination in mind. The sign she needed to see was less than a mile away. As she approached it, she pulled over, putting on her hazards. The sign in question showed that Bristol had a Rotary Club meeting every first and third Tuesday at eleven in the morning. The meetings took place at the Steadfast restaurant. When she last checked, the owner of the Steadfast, Mr. MacDunn, was also a Rotarian. It made sense for him to host the meetings, but it also meant a guaranteed check at an otherwise slow time of the week. He did have a reputation for being a good business-man, and this model seemed to fit the narrative.

Since Rebecca was the town's librarian, she knew several of the Rotarians on a first-name basis. She had donated to and volunteered at the Penny Sale, a fundraiser for the Rotary Club, for as long as she could remember and often allowed the group to host events in the multi-purpose room. It wouldn't be completely out of place for her to show up at their lunch meeting with a question or concern. Now, Rebecca just needed to come up with a plausible reason for showing up to a meeting where she wasn't on the agenda.

Chapter 5

The Lunch

Rebecca spent some time that morning at the library, checking in books and tidying up from the previous day's events. There wasn't much to do, so she spent most of the time checking the various clocks around the building. When it was close enough to eleven, she pulled out of the parking lot and headed east. The next parking lot she pulled into was nearly empty. She watched from her car to see if other patrons were entering. Not realizing that the restaurant might be closed to the public, she checked for their hours on her phone.

"Drat," she said to herself. While the Rotarians might have a meeting at eleven, the dining rooms wouldn't be open, nor would the ability to order a takeout lunch be possible. If she was going to do this, she'd have to think on her feet.

When Rebecca spotted a woman walking briskly to the front of the restaurant, she hopped out of her car to intercept her.

"Hey, Francine." She waved as she rounded the back end of her car.

The woman squinted and shielded her eyes, trying to identify the person who had called out to her. "Oh, hey, Rebecca. What are you doing here?"

"I know I didn't plan to attend, but I had a few questions for the group, if you think you might be able to sneak me in. It's totally informal information gathering, so I promise not to take much of your time."

Francine was a Friend of the Library and often participated in evening events by getting the multipurpose room ready, supplying food and drinks, and advertising. She hadn't been able to attend the event in March, when Jonah had spoken about working on Tattered Mountain, but was already preparing for an event in May.

"Let's see if we can't fit you in before we start the agenda. How was last month's event?"

"Um." Rebecca wasn't sure how to answer that. Had Francine not heard about what happened after Jonah had spoken? "The event itself went well. Great turnout. Still trying to figure out how to get more men to attend."

"Well, I'm sure you'll get there."

They stepped up to the front door together where Rebecca opened and held it for Francine to walk through, following immediately behind her. They walked with a purpose to the right and entered the tavern area of the building. There was a large table with several Rotarians already sitting around it.

"What have we here?" announced Morey Bourne, director of the Community Center.

"Just here to get some information. Not looking to crash the party." Rebecca scanned the members and didn't see anyone who might be a Nelson. "How are things at the Community Center?"

"We have hired a new assistant director, so that's good. Taking some work off my plate already."

"Fantastic." After the way the Father and Daughter Dance had gone before Valentine's Day, Rebecca was happy to hear things were looking up for Morey.

Francine sat at the table and invited Rebecca to sit with her. Looking over her shoulder at the front door, she declined. "I'm all set and don't intend to stay." She saw an elderly man enter and walk slowly into the tavern.

"Are we ready to get started?"

"Nelson," Francine acknowledged. "With you here, we are ready. Rebecca just had a few questions for us. I'm assuming they're about the library."

"They are, but I wanted to ask you, Nelson, how your brother is doing?"

He looked up at her, cranky and inquisitive at the same time. "My brother? Which one and how do you know him?" Was Nelson intentionally going to avoid identifying the brother who lived in the next town over, hopefully still fighting for his life?

"I'm asking about Joseph. Chief Towne and I were honored to have him show us the basics of making maple syrup on his property this past Sunday, but when I went back Monday after work, I found him lying on the floor of

41

his sugar shack. I was the one to call the ambulance, but I haven't heard if he survived. How is he?"

"He passed away last night. Thank you for asking." Nelson didn't shed a tear, nor did his voice break. The declaration that he no longer had Joseph in his life, his younger brother, seemed to not impact him whatsoever.

"Nelson, I'm so sorry." This was followed by a chorus of Rotarians also giving their condolences and asking what he needed. "Were you able to see your brother before he passed away?" Rebecca was fishing for a timeline. She knew from Mrs. Josephson that Nelson, or someone named Nelson, had been to the house on Easter.

"I visited him on Sunday, but I didn't make it to the hospital before he passed away."

Again, people jumped in to comfort him.

"Let's not make a fuss of this. We're all old, and we're all going to die sometime. His time just happened to be yesterday." He motioned for everyone else to sit as he sat at the head of the table. "Can we bring this meeting to order or at least place our lunch orders?"

Mr. MacDunn, owner of The Steadfast and fellow Rotarian, motioned for the bartender to join them. "Let's order." He handed out papers with a modified menu on them. "And then we'll let Rebecca speak so she can get going. Want something for lunch?"

"I'd be foolish to turn it down. I was bummed to learn you weren't open for lunch today when I made the decision to stop by."

The Rotarians and Rebecca perused the paper menu with four choices. The bartender took orders around the table. When he got to Rebecca, she ordered the Chicken Bacon Ranch Wrap. It was easy to transport and eat, and it would be good even if she didn't get to it right away. "I'll have mine for takeout, if that's okay," she said to the bartender. He nodded.

Mr. MacDunn spoke up. "So, Rebecca, what was it you came here to speak to us about today?"

She had forgotten completely to come up with a story before she entered The Steadfast. "Well, you see..." Why was she here? What could she possibly need so quickly she couldn't just wait to be put on the agenda for another meeting. "I'm sorry I can't keep a thought straight. Nelson, your brother's passing really hits home. The girls who were there with me were just taken by the process of making maple syrup and Mr. Josephson's kind nature. You were fortunate to have each other for so long."

"He was a right stick in the mud, he was. Didn't want to update his system. Our parents left him the house and the property with all those trees. Man was sitting on a gold mine and didn't want to make the most of it. It was being wasted on nostalgia."

"I'm assuming his wife will keep the house and property now, right?" This could be motive. With Joseph out of the way, did Nelson stand a chance at getting his hands on the family farm?

"As far as I understand, the farm has to stay in the family, blood that is. I'm the oldest living sibling, so I believe it will come to me."

The table was silent. Rebecca was silent. The only

sounds to be heard were taps and bangs in the kitchen, but that was dull background noise.

Francine, ever the diplomat, stood and took over. "Nelson, we'll help out in any way we can. Please know that everyone here supports you." He gave a curt nod. "What was it you came to ask about, Rebecca?"

"A generator. I believe the library needs a generator. I didn't budget for one for this year, but as a safe space in town, I believe we need to make sure there are public places the community members can go when the power goes out. I'm not sure how to make that happen before the snow flies this coming winter, so I figured I would come to you for suggestions and possibly support."

Morey asked, "Where did this come from?"

"You know, I was speaking with Fitch at Always-Starts back at the Haunted Hike in October about getting a generator for the library, then never acted on it. We got lucky this winter, but I don't want to risk it. Do you think it's even possible to entertain the idea of getting one so quickly?"

The Rotarians looked at each other, no one wanting to speak first. Finally, Morey responded, "I don't want to speak prematurely or for the group, but we can discuss our budget as well as opportunities we know of for grants and such and get back to you after the next meeting. How does that sound?"

"Would that be after the third Tuesday of the month?" She wanted to get the timing right to make her story seem more believable, especially since she had just looked at the sign earlier this morning.

"That's correct. One of us will contact you when we have either numbers or suggestions." Morey's face scanned the other Rotarians who verbally agreed with single-syllable responses.

The bartender reemerged with a container and handed it to Rebecca. "How much do I owe you?" She fumbled to get her wallet out of her pocket because she was now balancing the container in one hand.

"It's on me. We appreciate all you do in the community," was Mr. MacDunn's response.

"That's so sweet. Thank you so much."

"And thank you. I heard good things about your April Fool's event. Make sure to put that on your annual calendar."

"Absolutely. It's one of my favorite holidays. Thanks again." She lifted the lunch container in Mr. MacDunn's direction. No one stood as she exited, and she heard the meeting commence on her way out.

Setting the lunch down on the passenger seat, she gathered her thoughts. Nelson believes he is getting the farm. What does he expect Mrs. Josephson to do, move out? If he's retired, he must already have somewhere else he's living. Would he even want the farm? It's not like he can manage any of it. Rebecca had watched him struggle just to walk. She couldn't imagine him tapping all of the trees then lugging the sap back to the sugar shack. He had been so dismissive, disappointed even, in his brother for keeping with the old ways of maple sugaring, she was sure he wouldn't put in the work to keep that part of the farm operational. Before starting the car, she took out her phone and dialed Kenny's number, putting it on speaker.

She put the car in reverse to get out of her parking space then pulled forward and took a right turn out of the parking lot while the phone rang. "Is it a motive if he can't really use the farm?" she asked herself.

"Hello, Chief Towne."

"Don't even recognize my phone number anymore because it's been so long?"

"I'm sorry. I didn't even look at the number when I accepted the call. What's up?" His voice sounded distant, distracted.

"I spoke to Nelson, Joseph's brother. He told me Joseph Josephson passed away last night."

"I wanted to tell you, but I didn't know yet if his family had been notified. How did you happen to run into him?"

Rebecca could feel her cheeks go pink with heat. Luckily, Kenny couldn't see them. "Happen is a funny word. If by happen you mean, how did I learn he had a brother that was also a Rotarian and that they had a meeting this morning at The Steadfast, I would tell you I did some research last night."

"Very impressive."

"I was trying to remember the names last night that Mrs. Josephson had rattled off to Officer Adams, and Nelson was one of them. He had eight siblings, and an old article online mentioned their names. I put the rest together enough to *happen* to talk to Nelson this morning," she told Kenny as she drove.

"You got to him before I did, so anything I should know?"

"Turns out, he believes he's getting the family farm over Mrs. Josephson. I found that very interesting."

"So do I. What made him think that? Most people would assume the spouse would get it."

"He said it was something from their parents that if the one who owns the farm dies it goes to another blood relative in the family. Now, depending on the timeline, he had opportunity and motive." Rebecca smiled, proud of herself.

"We haven't nailed down a full timeline yet because we have interviews remaining, but I agree it's not looking good for Nelson at the moment."

"Can you tell me if you're investigating a murder or an accident?"

"Which one do you think we should be investigating." She could just imagine the smug look on his face.

"Last time I checked, doors like the one on the sugar shack don't lock themselves. I'm guessing you're investigating this murder syrup-titiously."

Chapter 6

The Update

They ended the call as Rebecca entered the center of town. Though it wasn't time for the library to open yet, she had some more online investigating to do. With her choice of parking spots open, she backed into one closest to the road. The flashbacks of finding Jeremy lying on the ground meant she'd never park in the same spot again.

There were no new books in the drop box, and everything was in order for the start of the day, so she turned on the computer in the office to figure out who either Warren or Bobby were. The library had a database for anyone who had ever taken out a library card, and there were only three men named Warren. Making a few assumptions, Rebecca figured she would start with a man named Warren Mitchell who lived on the town line between Bristol and Hill. Once she had a name, she started searching online for any information about Mr. Mitchell.

As it turned out, Mr. Mitchell also had a maple syrup business along with his own farm. According to an article from two years ago, he had done all of the updating that Joseph wasn't interested in doing. The pictures showed the gravity-fed tubing system he put in place during the previous summer and the collection barrels. His claim was that the profits would pay off the upgrades in less than five years.

Rebecca checked the clock, did the mental math, and took off for the front door. She left the computer on, locked up and raced for her car. The drive to Warren's farm was under ten minutes. He had a state-of-the-art building that could have been a home. When she pulled into the parking lot, she noticed they were still in the swing of things as far as turning sap into syrup. There was currently a truck with a large tank in the back depositing sap into a holding tank on the outside of the building.

"Excuse me," Rebecca said as she walked in the direction of the building. "Is Mr. Warren Mitchell here?"

The tall man who appeared to be in his early twenties responded, "He's inside," and went straight back to work.

Rebecca entered through the front door with an open sign displayed in the window and a hand-carved sign that read Sugarmakers. If she thought the outside of the structure was stunning, the inside was opulent. The vaulted ceiling with exposed beams screamed money. Everything in the center of the room was silver and polished to a white-glove standard. There were knobs and tubes and pipes and vats weaving magically throughout the space.

A door at the back of the room swung open, and a sturdy man with a full salt-and-pepper beard walked toward Rebecca wearing a red and black checkered flannel shirt and Carhartt work pants. "How can I help you?"

"I'm looking for Warren Mitchell. My name's Rebecca Ramsey, and I am the librarian in town."

"Good morning, afternoon, which is it?" he said in a gruff tone but with a friendly smile.

"Just past noon."

"Well, good afternoon. And why do I have the pleasure of your visit today? Are you interested in shopping? We have everything maple syrup you could hope for, including baked goods, cookbooks and novelties." He sure came off as a good people-person.

"Mr. Mitchel, I'm..."

He cut her off. "Please, call me Ren. Everyone does."

"Okay. Ren, I'm looking for some maple butter. Is that something you make?"

He escorted her by the elbow over to the refrigerated case. She couldn't decide if this was endearing or cringeworthy. "Darling, we have maple butter in two different sizes, and it freezes well too. I know Vermont thinks they hold the market on creamees, but we also have maple creamee by the pint with or without maple candies. Just let me know if there's anything you can't find."

"Will do." She opened the cooler door and selected a tub of maple butter. "Mr. Mitchell, I mean, Ren, did you hear about Mr. Josephson? I assume those of you in the business know each other." If she wasn't mistaken, there was a slight hesitation as if he was processing what she said before he spoke.

"Um, I'm sorry, but I'm not sure what you're referring to. I guess I don't really consider him to be 'in the business' as you called it. I mean, we both make maple syrup, but I'm the only businessman out of the two of us."

Now she paused. "Are you friends? Acquaintances?"

"I'd say closer to acquaintances than friends, but why do you ask?"

The idea that he wouldn't know was so completely outside how she thought this interaction was going to go; it caught her off guard instead of her catching him off guard. "So, Mr. Josephson, Joseph Josephson, passed away."

"Are you sure?"

She was stunned by the response, as if she was about to yell out 'April Fools!' after getting a reaction out of him. "Of course I'm sure. First of all, I found him in his sugar shack after being locked in it for some time, and I followed up and learned he later died at the hospital."

He touched the corner of his left eye and sniffed. "He was a good man, Mr. Josephson. Old fashioned 'til the end, but always a good man."

"Seems like maybe more than just acquaintances."

"We didn't see each other often, but when we did, we'd catch up with a long conversation over coffee."

"Odd, though, because Mrs. Josephson said on

Monday that you stopped by on Easter. That was just two days ago, and a holiday. What did you stop by for?"

He quickly responded, "I just had to drop off something I borrowed. Didn't even see Joseph."

"Well, that makes sense." But it didn't. Why drive out there, on Easter, with bad roads, to drop something off to a man who wasn't doing this as a business, just a hobby. She really wanted to ask what it was, but that would be too suspicious. "I guess I'll take the maple butter."

Mr. Warren walked over to the register to ring up her purchase. "Are you sure you don't want to get some maple candy as well, or fresh New Hampshire maple syrup?" He held up a glass bottle in the shape of a maple leaf.

"I think this will be good. I got maple syrup from Mr. Josephson on Easter. I'm pretty sure we were there earlier than you that day. Any idea what time you stopped by?"

"After noon some time. Maybe three. I guess I don't really know. Easter's not a big deal to me. Once church is over, there's no big family anything. Not married. No kids. It's just another day of work in the middle of my busiest time of the year because it was so early this year."

Rebecca paid for her maple butter and accepted the change from her twenty. "I'm going to stop by with food for Mrs. Josephson. I'm sure this has been really hard on her." Rebecca turned to leave and had reached the door when Warren responded.

"I wouldn't be so sure of that."

"Why not?" Rebecca wasn't sure that Mrs. Josephson

would be all that broken up over losing her husband based on her reaction that day, but she was hoping to get more information from Warren if there was any to be acquired.

"They were basically roommates. I'm sure it'll be weird that he's gone, but it was a marriage of convenience at this point. Not trying to start rumors or disparage anyone's memory, but it's just how things were."

"Do you think she'll keep the farm or sell it?"

He pondered the question, pulling at his beard. "I'm guessing she'll stay. It's what she knows. I mean, they've lived there together at least the last twenty years, maybe more."

"I can see how moving at her age would be challenging." She pushed on the door. "I'm sure I'll be back again." Holding the maple butter up as a wave, she left.

"I hope so," he called out before the door closed.

Rebecca wondered if he was covering for something. He returned an item but didn't see Mr. Josephson, but Mrs. Josephson knew he had been there. What did that mean?

Checking her watch, she knew she'd make it back to the library before opening, but it left her with a large part of her day occupied. She did try to remind herself that running the library was her actual job, not the sleuthing she enjoyed so much.

Mary was in the parking lot when Rebecca pulled in. She had half forgotten she was coming in. The two walked from their cars to the front doors together.

"Why aren't you getting the books from the drop box?" Mary asked.

"I've already been here twice today."

"Twice, before opening? What's going on?"

They assumed their positions behind the checkout desk, Mary's cardigan now hanging on the back of her swivel chair.

"First, how was your Easter?" Rebecca inquired.

"The service was lovely, and I had Easter supper with some of the ladies I attend with."

"That sounds nice."

"How was yours? How did your family decide to schedule the day?" Mary had attended this past Thanksgiving with Rebecca, Kenny, the girls, Jeremy and Kenny's ex-wife with her boyfriend. She was well aware that they were all on good terms.

"The girls attended church with Heather and Kenny, then just the four of us went to Hill to get a lesson on making maple syrup."

"That sounds delightful, dear. Where did you go for that?"

She gave a tight smile and took a long inhale and exhale. "Well, we went to Mr. Joseph Josephson's home quite a way out on Borough Road, and he showed us the taps and buckets and how to boil the sap in the sugar shack. The girls had a great time."

"So, why the long pause before telling me that?"

"When we were ready to leave, Mr. Josephson sent us home with maple syrup. I returned the next day to give him money, and I found him locked in the sugar shack with almost no pulse. I learned later that he died in the hospital. It was a horrible discovery and then for him to end up dying after I was the one calling for an ambulance was just double tough. We didn't tell the girls because they'd have no reason to ever run into him again, but we know."

"You poor thing. I suppose you're already working on something. I did hear you say he was locked in the sugar shack."

"I don't have anything official, but my guess is he died from smoke inhalation. When I opened the door, a huge cloud of smoke billowed out of the open doorway, practically knocking me over. He'd have been trapped in there, breathing that, or attempting to breathe."

"That just doesn't add up. I'm sure he had a chimney for exactly that reason. Why would all the smoke have built up? Has anyone inspected the chimney?"

Rebecca thought about it. "I don't know, but I'll pass that along to Kenny or Jacob. If someone tampered with the chimney, there might be prints. Good thinking, Mary. You are always so logical."

"You are too, dear, but you experienced the whole situation and probably recall the facts layered with the emotion. I wasn't there, so I can hear only facts."

"And I'm very glad to have you to toss ideas around with. Now we just need to figure out how to find the last person to interview."

"Last person? How long have you been at this?" Mary's eyes were round with awe. "It's only Tuesday, and you said this happened yesterday?"

"Off the bat, I have three people of interest. I've talked to two already, and I want to get back out to talk to Mrs. Josephson after I find the final person of interest."

"Do you have a name?"

"Bobby, but that's not much to go on."

"I can see someone about to come into the library." Mary pointed in the direction of the parking lot. "Let's get them in and out quickly so we can get to work on figuring out who Bobby is."

Chapter 7

The Wife

WHEN THE PATRON HAD LEFT WITH THEIR RESERVED book, Mary started searching in the library's computer.

"That won't be much help. There are too many people with the name Bobby, and we don't know if that's what would be on their library card anyway. They could be Robert on their license but Bobby to friends."

"Well, did you try?" Mary asked.

"I tried searching for Bobby in Bristol and Bobby in Hill on a search engine, but there were too many results."

Mary placed her reading glasses on her nose and tapped away at the keyboard. "Nothing is standing out, but let's try that search engine thing again. Can you pull it up?"

Rebecca scooted her chair over next to Mary's. She opened a search engine and typed in 'Bobby Bristol New Hampshire' then clicked the search button.

Mary waved her hand. "We already know that didn't

work, so let's try 'Bobby Joseph Josephson New Hampshire' to see if there is anything with both names."

Rebecca was shocked she hadn't thought of that. The very first link showed a match. "I stand corrected," clarified Rebecca. "What did you find?"

Mary clicked on the link and found an article about several family farms in New Hampshire that had spanned over two hundred years. The Josephson farm was one. "Looks like you have a family connection here."

Rebecca read the start of the article to herself and learned that Mr. and Mrs. Josephson had a son named Bobby. "Well, I didn't see that coming. At no point did Mr. Josephson mention a son, nor did I see any evidence of him when I was in their house to call for the ambulance."

"There was no reason for you to know, but now you do. Let's search for him." Rebecca and Mary learned that Bobby was Mr. Josephson's son who lived in New York.

"If he lives in New York, why would he just stop by on Easter leaving Mrs. Josephson to say she might have seen his truck. We're talking about someone who would have to have driven over two hours minimum to just stop by and only see one parent. That just doesn't add up."

Rebecca resigned herself to the fact that she wouldn't be making any more progress today on this case. She and Mary talked about niceties like the weather and what their plans were for future gardening projects. When Mary left after a few hours of volunteering, Rebecca was alone for the rest of the evening. Since it was the only day of the week the library was open late, she saw several of the regulars, people who couldn't come to the earlier hours on other days, and people who just came in often regardless of the day of the week. With nothing else exciting happening, she locked up and went home to her fur babies.

Entering her home, no one greeted her at the door. When she had removed her shoes and entered the kitchen, prepared to feed two very hungry kitties, only Bean was visible. "Where's Joey?" she asked, waiting for Bean to show her the way as if Lassie were in the kitchen instead. Rebecca looked up to see the door to the basement was open a crack. "Great." She went about putting wet food in the dishes and even shook a container of cat treats, trying to entice Joey to come back upstairs, but it was all for nothing. When the cats took advantage of an unsecured door, she didn't typically see them for hours.

She hadn't heard much from Kenny since the day after Easter when she left the Josephson farm. He must have been out straight with the investigation and the girls, so she'd give him another day before giving him a hard time.

Her bed looked welcoming after a full morning of investigating and a day of work at the library. She plugged her phone into the charger at her nightstand, checking one last time to see if Kenny had sent her a message – he hadn't. After her quick bathroom routine, she drifted off to sleep, this time without the waking dreams of finding Jeremy in the parking lot, and didn't rouse until her cats jumped on her sometime around dawn. She tossed and turned, trying to go back to sleep, but failed.

"Fine, I'll get up." When she sat up, they jumped down from the bed and waited in her bedroom doorway. She went downstairs, closed the basement door, and changed their water then added dry food to their bowls when an idea hit her.

Rebecca decided to go see Mrs. Josephson. It was unlikely she'd be able to track down Bobby if he did return to New York after Easter, but his mother would be easier to ask a few more questions of. Before she could just show up on her doorstep, there needed to be a plan explaining why she was there.

Checking her phone for a recipe, she located one for a cookie called a mapledoodle; it followed the general recipe for a snickerdoodle but was a maple-flavored cookie that still required cream of tartar. She took out two sticks of unsalted butter and placed them upright, not lying down, in the middle of her stovetop. She gathered two pint glasses from her cabinet and filled them with hot water. After a couple minutes had passed while she was petting her cats, she emptied the glasses and turned them over, covering the sticks of butter with the warm glass. This trick was something she found one night while scrolling through her phone to soften butter without melting it in the microwave.

Rebecca went back upstairs to shower and get ready for the day, returning to the kitchen to find the butter was the perfect consistency for making cookies. She pulled out her stand mixer, extra bowls and utensils to make the cookies she now planned to bring to Mrs. Josephson. The snickerdoodle recipe, with bonus ingredients, was easy to make and easily baked up in about thirty-five minutes total, leaving her an annoying amount of time to kill before she could reasonably show up at the Josephson Farm.

When she decided she had waited as late as possible to still have time to get out to Hill and back before opening the library, she gathered up the sugar-covered cookies to deliver.

Since it was still cold in the evening and warmer during the day, she suspected sap was still flowing. Rebecca wasn't shocked to see a lack of smoke rising from the sugar shack chimney. She parked in the driveway, next to a truck she didn't recognize, and got out, keeping an eye on the sugar shack on her walk up to the front door. When Mrs. Josephson answered, she still had her head turned to the left.

The woman who answered the door had on her robe and slippers, just like the last time she had been there. "Morning, Mrs. Josephson," she said, purposefully leaving off the word good. "I brought you some maple snickerdoodles and hoped maybe you had time to chat before I need to get to work. I'm sorry for your loss."

Without verbally responding, Mrs. Josephson opened the front door wide enough to let Rebecca in. She led the way to the living room where a game show was on the television screen. "What can I do for you?"

"I just wanted to check in. How are you doing?"

"I've been better." She stared at the television screen as she answered Rebecca.

"I heard that Mr. Josephson passed away later that night, after I found him. Do you have help with all of the paperwork you'll need to do in order to, well, settle things." Rebecca wasn't sure of the proper wording and didn't think it mattered much to Mrs. Josephson in the moment.

"Joseph's son is here to help with things."

Rebecca knew that there was at least one son named Bobby, but the way she referred to him was odd. "Joseph's son? Who might that be?"

"Bobby came back when he heard what happened."

"I've never met your son before. I'd like to at least give my condolences if he's available."

She finally turned to look at Rebecca. "He's not my son. Bobby was Joseph's son from his first marriage. My kids are grown and live in Maine and Vermont."

"Oh. I didn't realize that. So, Bobby stopped by on Easter? Where does he live?"

Mrs. Josephson turned back to the game show, but it was now on a commercial. "Bobby lives in New York with his family, but he drove over to see his father on Easter, at least I assumed it was his truck in the driveway. I already told the police he was here the same as Nelson and Warren."

"In that order?" Rebecca was pressing her luck, but the way the widow was staring at the screen, she hoped the answer would be automatic instead of thought provoking.

"I don't remember what order they were here. I know Joseph was looking forward to seeing your family for a little tour. Made him happy. Visitors were not expected otherwise, so I didn't pay much attention. I know I heard Warren, saw Nelson and I'm pretty sure Bobby's truck was in the driveway at some point. Joseph was so busy with maple syrup, I never saw him again after you guys left. I never got to say goodbye, and he died in that darn sugar shack alone." She finally broke, tears streaming silently down her face.

Rebecca waited a moment before standing and going over to hug Mrs. Josephson. It felt awkward, but she grasped Rebecca's arm back and didn't let go for a long time. It was a passing thought from years ago, but she remembered hearing that whoever the hug was for should be the person to end it, so she let Mrs. Josephson hold the hug as long as necessary. "I'm better now," she said as she let go and wiped the tear tracks from her face.

"Can you remember anything else from Sunday?"

"I've really told you and the police everything I can remember."

"I'm sure you have." Rebecca needed to shift the conversation before she attempted to talk to Bobby. "With Mr. Josephson gone, will you continue to live here? I know family farms often try to stay in the family, so I didn't know what that meant in your case."

"Do you mean there is a chance I won't just automatically keep my house?"

Rebecca knew she was stirring the pot, but figured Mrs. Josephson was the person most likely to have had real details regarding a will or trust for Joseph and the farm.

"I'm asking if you and Mr. Josephson had any kind of will drawn up to determine what happened to your assets in case the other died. If not, I think the standard is for things to go to the spouse, unless there is any other paperwork or agreements preceding the marriage."

"That's a new stress I didn't know I should be having. I've never gone to a lawyer before, and I don't know if Joseph did." She started to wring her hands. "I guess we can go out and ask Bobby what he knows."

The pair stood together.

"Let me go put some clothes on."

Mrs. Josephson left the living room and walked upstairs. Rebecca took the opportunity to look around the first floor. She found pictures of Mr. Josephson at different stages of his life. Sometimes he was with other men his age, other times a young boy, and one picture was with his current wife. Otherwise, it was a simple house with nothing particularly memorable.

When Mrs. Josephson returned, she was wearing jeans and a hooded sweatshirt. She looked younger out of the robe and slippers.

"Where should I leave the cookies?" Rebecca asked.

"Just on that side table is fine. I'll put them away when we come back in."

They walked outside and turned right to head toward the sugar shack.

"And you said his son's name is Bobby, correct?"

"Yes, named after Joseph's younger brother, Robert, who died when he was just a baby."

It seemed like every direction Rebecca turned, this family dynamic just got more and more complicated.

Mrs. Josephson opened the door to the sugar shack. "Bobby, there's someone here to see you."

Chapter 8

The Offspring

"BOBBY, MY NAME IS REBECCA RAMSEY. I WAS HERE on Easter to get lessons on making maple syrup from your father. I'm so sorry for your loss." Mrs. Josephson stood just outside the open door, holding it.

Bobby stood to full height and made eye contact with Rebecca. "I appreciate that. Why was it you were here on Easter? I didn't see you when I stopped by."

"We came after church to learn about the process of making maple syrup. Apparently, my fiancé knew your father well enough to ask the favor to make the day special for his two daughters."

"Sounds like Dad to do that. Maybe you can help me then. I haven't done this in some time. Dad had started a batch that was ruined when the ambulance took him because it boiled down too much. I've cleaned it all up, but something's not working right. Every time I start the fire, the whole room fills up with smoke. I had to keep the door propped open, but I know Dad never did that when he was boiling sap." Bobby's eyes looked glassy, and he had developed a nostalgic look. "I can remember how much I hated making maple syrup with Dad. My mother, when she was alive, would tell me that I'd remember those days fondly when I was grown, but I didn't believe her. Guess she was right."

"It's easy to know something like that when you're an adult. Believing it when you're a child is tricky. So, did you come back to finish the boiling season, is that why you're trying to get the fire started?"

"I think Dad would be sad if he knew any sap went to waste. There isn't much left at this point, season's almost over, so I figured I'd try to finish it up since I have to be here to help with lawyers and paperwork."

Rebecca's attention was diverted when Mrs. Josephson added, "Bobby and I have a meeting tomorrow. Some lawyer from Plymouth contacted me when they heard Joseph had passed away."

Turning her head back to Bobby, Rebecca asked, "Do you know what the will says, Bobby? Who gets the farm?"

"I have no idea. Men of Dad's generation never talked about that kind of stuff with their kids. Even if we were full grown with kids of our own, they always looked at us as their children." Bobby kept working under the pan for boiling the sap.

"What are you looking for?" Rebecca asked.

"I'm trying to figure out if something is stuck in here causing the smoke to build up and stay in the shack instead of going up through the chimney. I haven't been in here in probably thirty years, so I'm rusty."

Rebecca walked around the right side of the pan where she could access the chimney. "Bobby, I'm pretty sure this is your problem." She was attempting to move the damper, but it was stuck. "If you can't move this, you can't let the smoke out. I remember Joseph showing it to the girls."

Rebecca moved out of the way so she was standing in the doorway allowing Bobby to get around to that side of the space. "Rebecca, I think you're right. Why would it be stuck closed? If Dad had been in here boiling sap when he was found, this closed damper would have prevented smoke from getting out. He would have known better than to start a boil with a broken damper."

"When I found him, he was lying on the floor. He would have known there was too much smoke, but it must have been too late."

"Why not just leave? He should have had enough of a warning that the shack was filling up with smoke to get out."

Rebecca hesitated. She didn't know how much Bobby already knew and didn't look forward to being the one to tell him everything. "I showed up on Monday to give your father money for the syrup he gifted us. I know it wasn't necessary, but syrup is worth a lot, and it takes a lot of work to make what he sent us home with. When I didn't see smoke, I assumed he was in the house. I talked to your..." She took a long time to say the word your, hoping someone would fill in the missing detail.

"Stepmother," Bobby offered.

"Yes. I asked her where Joseph was, and she thought he was out here. I had to unlatch the door to get in and faced a plume of smoke before locating him on the floor. Bobby, I know the door was locked."

"There's no lock on the door. I've been telling him for years there is value in the equipment even when he's not boiling and should lock it up, but he never has."

She walked outside and motioned for him to do the same. When all three were outside the shack, she showed him the handle. "From the inside, this would have acted like a lock. I've been trying to piece it together, and from what I know, I think someone came here, broke the damper then left, virtually locking him in the room. With the shack being so old, windows just weren't a luxury his parents would have paid for. The last option would have been removing the hinge pins, but those are on the outside as well. At his age, breaking down the door probably wouldn't have worked either."

"But what about putting out the fire? Why not try to douse it with something?"

"As you said, the contents of the pan were beyond syrup when you had to clean it, so most of the moisture was probably already evaporated and wouldn't have done much to put out a fire. The other issue might have been creating more smoke. I'm not sure if there was any water or sap in here when I found him, but it might have felt like the safer gamble to wait out the fire on the floor with a handkerchief. It looked like he had been holding it, maybe to his face, and it fell out of his hand, maybe when he had breathed in too much smoke. If it had been wet, it might have helped. I'm sure the police took it as evidence. At least, I hope they did." Rebecca started to look around. "I don't see it in here anymore."

There was a muffled sound from behind them. Mrs. Josephson was crying again. This time, Bobby went to hold her. "I'm sure with Rebecca as the witness or whatever you want to call her, this will all get sorted. She seems to have her head screwed on straight. Do you work for the police?"

"My fiancé is the chief of police in Bristol, and he works on investigations like this. I'm a librarian."

"I didn't expect that. Either way, I'm glad you're on our side." Bobby continued to hold his stepmother.

Starting to feel like the third wheel, Rebecca checked the clock on her phone. She only had fifteen minutes to get to the library and have it open to the public.

"I'm so sorry to run, but I need to get to the library. I'll call Kenny, I mean, Chief Towne, and let him know what we've discovered today so he can come by and talk to you both and maybe collect more evidence. I'm hoping they'll have this solved in no time." She was walking briskly to her car when Bobby caught up to her.

"If you need me for anything, here's my number." He handed her his business card. "I know we're talking to the lawyer tomorrow morning, but I want to make sure you have access to whatever you need to find out what happened to my father. I don't want anyone getting their hands on money or property if they're the ones who did this." His face was stern but not angry.

"I'll do my best." She tried to sound reassuring without providing too much hope. She felt like she'd already uncovered a lot of details and talked to every one of her leads, but maybe Kenny would have something to go on, if he'd answer his phone.

Arriving at the library with one minute to spare, no one was waiting in the parking lot. She grabbed the books from the drop box and keyed in, leaving the books in a pile on the counter. She called Kenny's cell from hers and waited. It went to his voicemail. She ended the call without leaving a message and called him from the library phone. Again, he didn't answer. This time, she called the non-emergency number for the police station.

"Police station, Jenny speaking."

Jenny had been a library kid when Rebecca first started as the town's librarian. She was young but very responsible. Rebecca was proud of her for getting a job within the local law enforcement.

"Hey, Jenny, it's Rebecca Ramsey. I don't mean to bother you, but can you put me through to Chief Towne? He isn't answering his cell phone."

"Is this about the Josephson investigation?"

"What makes you think that?" Rebecca was curious.

"I was asked if you called the station to tell you that Jacob is heading up that investigation. Want to talk to him?"

She was hoping to talk to someone in person. "Can you tell Jacob that I have new details he will want to know? I'm at the library, and he should stop by as soon as possible."

"I can tell him, but you'll be able to talk to him sooner if I just put the call through."

"I understand, but it's so much easier in person. Thanks. Try to convince him it's urgent, will you?"

Jenny chuckled. "I've been trying to convince him to take me out on a date for weeks now, so I'm not sure I'm the right woman for the job, but I'll do what I can. Have a nice day." Her smile could be heard in her voice.

Rebecca didn't previously know Jenny was interested in Jacob, but that detail would need to wait for another time. Already behind on her work for the library, Rebecca got started with the books that needed to be checked back in and reshelved.

Jacob sauntered through the doors within the hour. "Jenny insisted that I needed to find time right away to come talk to you."

"Well, guess she's better at convincing you than she thought she was."

"Come again?" He furrowed his brow. "Convincing me about what?"

"I'm just going to get this out of the way so we can focus on what's important. Jenny likes you and wants you to ask her out. She's been dropping hints, and you're not picking them up. She's nice and smart and pretty. Ask the girl out on a date. Okay?"

Jacob's jaw hung slack. "Jenny likes me?"

"Seems like it. Now, let's move on. I was at the Josephson farm today and so was Joseph's son, Bobby. I explained to Bobby how the door to the sugar shack was locked when I got there and how I found his father. Kenny passed that along to you, right?"

"Yes, and we took pictures of the door as evidence. What else?"

"Do you also have the handkerchief that was found next to his hand? The EMTs might not have found it important, but I'm hoping you guys grabbed it to test it."

"Test it for what?"

"Well, evidence that Mr. Josephson had been breathing through it, maybe. I'm not even sure if that's a thing. But also to eliminate his dying from anything else like poison."

Jacob removed his small notepad and pencil, jotting down something. "Anything else you found today?" He kept his eyes on the paper.

"When Bobby got there, he decided to finish up boiling the sap for the season, whatever was left. He lit the fire, but the room kept filling with smoke. He couldn't figure out what was causing it, but I did with Mary's help."

Jacob looked up from the pad of paper. "What? Why was the room filling with smoke?"

"The damper had been tampered with. It was stuck in the closed position. Not that I didn't think so before, but this absolutely wasn't an accident or someone who closed the door behind them absentmindedly. This was intentional."

Chapter 9

The Tea

"Well, that is worth going back out to look at. I'll check with the other officers to see what they already collected for evidence on the handkerchief as well as anything to do with the chimney. I appreciate you letting me know, Rebecca, but remember not to get in the way of our investigation."

She held up the three-finger salute from back in her Girl Scout days and said, "I promise to never intentionally get in your way."

"I like how you threw in the word intentionally, just to give you an escape route incase you do get in our way."

In her very best impression of a southern belle, she slapped her hand over her heart and gasped. "Whatever do you mean to imply, young officer?"

"If you haven't noticed, I'm moving up. This is the first case I'm the lead investigator on. I appreciate your help, but please don't mess it up for me." He was pleading with her, not only with his words, but also his eyes.

"I won't. I promise. Now, go do your official investigating stuff. If you need anything, don't hesitate to ask."

"I'll try not to be offended." He turned around and walked out of the library.

With so much time left in the day, she decided to call Jeremy. That April Fool's Day prank would hopefully make for good blackmail now that she needed something from him. His phone rang and when Rebecca was about to give up, he answered. "Hello?"

"Jeremy, so glad you were able to answer the phone. How is your day going?" She laid on the sugary sweetness one could only get with pure New Hampshire maple syrup running through their blood.

"I'm doing well." There was a momentary pause. "It's Wednesday," Jeremy stated.

"Yes, it is."

"What are you calling me for?"

Rebecca plucked up every ounce of cunning she could muster over the phone. "I'm in a really tough spot, and I'd be forever grateful if you'd come in for an hour or two."

"Today? Now?"

"Seeing as how you scared me to death on my very favorite holiday, I figure you owe me at least that?"

Jeremy chuckled at the other end of the call. "Are you going to hold that over my head forever?"

"No. Just until next year when I can get you back. Until then, I'm going to lean into this for all it's worth."

"I just finished running. Let me take a shower, and I'll be right down."

Rebecca gave a small celebratory leap, her fiery hair flowing around her shoulders as she pumped her fist. Calming down before speaking, she said, "I'll see you soon. Thanks."

Rebecca went about cleaning and making sure all was in order before Jeremy got there so she could fly out the door upon his arrival. When he walked in, there was a flurry of hugs and air kisses and words of gratitude. Jeremy didn't get more than two syllables out before the doors to the library closed behind her on her way to the waiting Subaru.

"I'm going to need to get this washed," she noted after looking at the results of driving on Borough Road.

Her car took her directly to Jilly's, the iconic diner where she knew she could dig up the local dirt if there was any. She was there in time for lunch and, hopefully, for the owner and chef, Reese, to spill the tea.

As she entered, she was greeted by Kathy with a K. "Rebecca, you looking to have lunch?"

"I'm just going to take a place at the counter."

The small diner had tables with chairs, booths and spinning counter stools. When customers sat on the stools, they could see Reese working in the kitchen through the hole in the wall where she passed food from the kitchen to the restaurant. Rebecca waved as she sat, hoping to get Reese's attention.

"Hey, Rebecca. Good day?"

"It will be if I can get a chance to talk to you." There wasn't any time for her to beat around the bush.

"Come back."

As quickly as Rebecca sat down, she jumped right back up at the invitation. When she entered the kitchen through the swinging saloon doors, she made sure to prioritize her time. "Can I order a chicken finger sandwich and fried pickles?"

"Glad to see that's all it takes for you to be happy."

"Not what I came for, but my time is short, and I need to bring lunch back to the library with me. "

"If you didn't come for the sandwich and pickles, what did you come for?" Reese stopped moving, which made an impact on Rebecca because Reese never stopped moving.

"I came to see what you know and what you've heard about Joseph Josephson's death and his family farm." Reese looked like she was about to protest before Rebecca held up her hand. "Don't even tell me you don't know anything about that family. Between your job here and the fact you live further up on the same road, there is no question in my mind you have some theories."

Reese went back to efficiently and elegantly making the food for the next ticket. "I'm not going to say I know nothing, but what I've heard isn't necessarily fact."

"I can work with that. What have you heard that might be true?"

"I stopped by to talk to Mrs. Josephson and see if she needed anything. Her son, Paul, was there."

"Wait, her son not his son? I met Bobby, Joseph's son,

and she was quick to let me know Bobby wasn't her son and that her two children live out of state."

"Technically, yes. Paul lives in Vermont, but you can get there in under two hours. He pops over for the day pretty often."

Rebecca found that interesting. "I'm not going to say she lied, but she certainly didn't volunteer that information. What else?"

"We never see the sister who lives in Maine, but I've wondered since Joseph passed away if Paul is going to move in with his mother."

"Why would he do that? Based on her age, I'd assume he'd already have a place of his own."

"Order up," hollered Reese through the pass. "The rumor is, he wants to take over the farm and run it, get rid of the animals and update the maple syrup production to be more of a business."

"Joseph would have been sad to learn that. He was so proud of how he hadn't caved to all the modern ways of others in the sugaring business. It was pride in a job well done that kept him going."

"I agree. I'd hate to see Paul get that farm, but I don't think that can happen."

"Why do you say that? Isn't it pretty standard for the spouse to keep the property. If she is the owner, there's nothing to stop her from moving her son in to run the place, regardless of how Joseph would have felt about his own son never getting the opportunity to run the family farm."

"Anyone on Borough Road knows the stories about

that farm. Something about it needing to stay in the family. If someone dies, it can't go to the spouse outside the bloodline. As far as I know, it's always gone to a male." Reese appeared to be working on Rebecca's chicken finger sandwich and fried pickles.

"That's pretty cool and pretty awful at the same time. Think about Mrs. Josephson. Where is she going to move to? It's not really fair to marry someone, move in with them, live a life with them and get kicked out of your home because they died. I mean, it's not like they got a divorce."

"Completely unfair, but I'm betting she doesn't know about it."

"Who is going to tell her?" Rebecca gasped. "There's a meeting tomorrow with the lawyers. I'm guessing she'll find out then. I get the history and wanting to keep the farm in the family, but she'll, what, move in with one of her kids? She's retired."

Reese boxed up the sandwich and fried pickles, handing them to Rebecca in a plastic bag. "Here you go. I'm sure whatever happens tomorrow at that meeting will be spilled across town by nightfall. Small town gossip spreads fast."

Rebecca internalized that as a challenge to figure things out before tomorrow's meeting. "Thanks making my lunch. I'll go back out to the front to pay. Have a great day, and let me know if you hear anything more, will ya?"

"Sure thing."

Rebecca passed through the swinging doors to the

restaurant side of the wall. She stepped up to the register at the start of the counter, waiting to pay whichever waitress stopped for her first.

"You all set?" hollered Kathy from the front of the diner.

"Yes, just need to pay."

Kathy walked over and started looking around. "She give you a bill?"

"No. I have a chicken finger sandwich and fried pickles."

Reese called from the kitchen, "It's on the house. Go solve that mystery." She waved, smiled and put her head down, working hard as always.

"Thanks!" Rebecca called back. "Have a nice day, Kathy."

"What mystery you working on now?" she asked.

"Mr. Josephson died out in Hill. I'm just trying to connect some dots."

"Seriously? Why are you trying to help him?"

Rebecca was shocked. "He was such a nice man. Why wouldn't I try to help his family figure out who killed him?"

"Ugh, he was always showing up to all the town meetings, trying to get the budget cut, or shut down the elementary school. Last time, you'd think he was in front of the Senate showing them what a filibuster was."

"What was the topic up for debate?"

"Something about private property. Specifically, it had something to do with hunting, but the way he was carrying on, I assumed there was something bigger that I was missing. Like a joke I wasn't part of."

"That's odd. I wonder if he's had trespassers on his property. Hunters sometimes go where they shouldn't. Could just have been about hunting and nothing more."

"I guess so, but he was really passionate about it, whatever he was ranting about. Most people left because he just kept going on and on."

"Isn't there a time limit?"

"For everyone else, yes. For a Josephson, there are different rules."

Rebecca paused. "How so?"

Kathy checked on one of her tables. "Be right there." Turning back to Rebecca, she whispered, "Their family was a big deal several generations ago, back when Hill was still called New Chester. They started the farm and provided a lot of the vegetables and dairy products to members of the community as they moved to the area and started up their own farms. Everyone bowed down to them and looked the other way if any one of them did something wrong. The offspring came to expect the same treatment, even though the farm had been reduced to a postage stamp. Back when more of Joseph's generation was still living in town, they acted like they ran the place. Ridiculous if you ask me." Kathy started to move toward her table. "Gotta go. See you later."

"Thanks for the information." Rebecca was convinced Kathy hadn't heard her, but there was no chance to try again once Kathy started talking to her customers.

The drive back to the library was short and set Rebecca's head whirling. When she entered, Jeremy was sitting behind the counter.

"What, not lying on the floor when you saw me pull in?"

"I can't say the thought didn't cross my mind, but I like working here. I'm not sure with your newly developed skill set, you couldn't make me disappear if necessary."

Rebecca put her lunch up on the check-out counter. "I hadn't thought about it, but I do have a very particular set of skills now."

"And what skills are you using today?"

Rebecca unboxed her sandwich and took a bite of the bread, chicken and cranberry sauce. "I'm thinking I need to look up the notes from a particular town meeting to get some details. You in?"

"Absolutely."

Chapter 10

The Evidence

Rebecca and Jeremy started to search for publicly available notes from the last town meeting that Kathy may have been referring to, and they found what they were looking for with no problem.

"Looks like Mr. Joseph Josephson was trying to support a vote preventing people from accessing private land, even if it wasn't for hunting."

"Isn't that just common sense? There are rules for posted land where you put signs up every so many feet and people aren't allowed to trespass."

"Of course they aren't allowed to, but who is going to stop them when the person who owns the land is anti-technology and doesn't have any way to check most of their property because of how far it is from their house."

"Are you saying Mr. Josephson thought someone was trespassing, but he didn't have proof?" Jeremy asked.

"I'm actually guessing he did have proof but needed

some kind of new regulation passed to do anything with the information he had."

"What kind of information do you think he had?"

Rebecca smirked. "If you can stay here for the rest of those two hours I asked for, I may be able to check on a hunch.

Jeremy agreed, and Rebecca was off again, this time to return to Hill to visit Mrs. Josephson. The day had started to warm up, and Rebecca was hopeful the ruts would be in her favor. The Subaru was all-wheel drive, but every low vehicle had its limitations.

By the grace of the maple syrup fairies, she made it up Borough Road, far enough to pull into the Josephson's driveway. If she had needed to make it all the way to Reese's house, she was confident it would have taken a tow truck to get her back out.

Stepping up to the front door, she was surprised to see a man she didn't know exiting the sugar shack.

"Good afternoon. I'm Rebecca Ramsey. I was coming to ask Mrs. Josephson if I could take a look at something."

"She's out right now. Could I help you? Name's Paul."

Rebecca's face lit up. "Oh, her son. Nice to finally meet you, though I only just learned about you today."

"Nice to meet you too. What was it you wanted to see?"

Rebecca explained what it was she thought might be happening and the location of the property she most wanted to look at. Since Paul hadn't been there before, he accompanied her. Less than thirty minutes later, Rebecca was back in her car and on the phone with Jacob as soon as cell phone service returned.

"Can you meet me there?" she asked. "I have some questions, and I think it might be best if someone else was there to hear the answers.

The next thing Rebecca did was pull into the parking lot of Sugarmakers.

Deciding not to wait in her car, she entered the beautiful space, pretending to examine the contents of the store.

"Back so soon?" The man with the salt-and-pepper beard sauntered toward her, this time wearing a green and black checkered flannel shirt.

"I couldn't stop thinking about the creamees. I wanted to bring some home for dessert."

"Of course you do." He had a smug smile she could easily make out through the beard.

"I had a question for you."

Jacob entered the building, tipping his hat at Warren and proceeding to look around the store as if shopping.

"Shoot. What's the question?"

"What was the item you borrowed from Mr. Josephson and returned on Easter?"

He looked up, stroking his facial hair with his hand. "It was a hydrometer. Measures the amount of moisture remaining in the syrup so you know when it's done."

"And that's something you borrowed from him?"

"Something happened to mine, and he was the closest person I could think of who might have one."

Rebecca took her phone out of her back pocket and

pulled up a photo, turning the screen to face Warren. "Is this it?"

He looked down his nose at the photo. "I believe it is. Why?"

"There's not a single piece of equipment in that sugar shack that looks like it was purchased since the year two thousand. This hydrometer is shiny and brand new. Why would he have such a new piece of equipment available to loan to you?"

"I'm not sure. Maybe his broke, and he bought a new one."

"Unfortunately, that doesn't hold water. Easter morning, he showed us how he used a rule of thumb to measure the moisture without any instruments, but he did have an old hydrometer hanging on the wall to the left of the chimney. I took this picture this morning, and this hydrometer is hanging on the right side of the chimney. Odd, don't you think?"

Every so often, Rebecca caught a glimpse of Jacob wandering around by the cookbooks and novelties.

"Okay, I'll change the subject. When did you start stealing sap from the maple trees on the back side of Mr. Josephson's property?"

"If you're going to accuse me of being a thief, I think you can take your business elsewhere."

"I'll ask the question then," Jacob interjected. "When did you start stealing sap from Mr. Josephson's maple trees?"

"That's preposterous. I'd never..."

"Before you say anything else, please understand that

we have the notes from the last town meeting where Mr. Josephson was in favor of stricter rules about trespassing, and you were in attendance to speak against them."

This time, Rebecca spoke. "I looked into your business, and you own land on both sides of the town line. You happen to own the land that abuts the back of Mr. Josephson's property, do you not?"

"That doesn't mean or prove anything," Warren defended.

"I walked out there with Paul, Mrs. Josephson's son, today and found that the trees Joseph had been tapping were only about ten trees deep into the woods. He had a huge forest of maple trees just sitting there, waiting to earn money. I'm willing to bet, you've previously, maybe even on Easter, made an offer to buy the farm from Mr. Josephson and he turned you down."

"Well, I..."

"I'm not finished. I'm also willing to bet when the police inspect the piece of the damper that had been broken off, causing the shack to fill with smoke and ultimately kill Mr. Josephson, will have your prints or DNA on it. That gift of a hydrometer, not a return, was the excuse to get into the shack and close enough to the damper to damage it.

"He was letting that forest go to waste in the name of the Josephson family. I didn't want to take the farm or even own part of the unused property, just the rights to tap the trees on the property, the ones he wasn't using."

"I take it," started Jacob, "that he didn't see it the same way."

"He said it would be stealing, and he was never going to let me use the land or buy the land. I figured if one of the kids, Bobby or Paul, got ahold of the property, they'd sell or lease at least the wooded part to me for quite the profit, for them and me."

"In case you didn't know, no one knows for sure who is getting the property. There is a meeting with a lawyer tomorrow, but it looks like either his brother Nelson or his son Bobby will get it. From what I've gathered, neither would be willing to sell. If you'd kept your mouth closed, maybe you could have gotten away with stealing the sap from a couple rows of trees for years. Years!" she emphasized.

"Look, I'm just building my brand here. Just getting started."

Jacob walked over, "And now that you're under arrest for the murder of Joseph Josephson, that brand is coming to a swift end."

He didn't fight being put into handcuffs and escorted to the back of a waiting cruiser. When Rebecca followed them out, she saw Kenny was in the driver's seat. He stepped out and met her in the middle of the dirt lot.

"Where have you been?" she asked incredulously. She smacked the side of his arm and pouted.

"I had all the faith in the world you and Jacob could solve this one on your own, well, together. I had another investigation that was going to take up all of my time, and he was ready. So were you. I knew it wasn't me helping you on all those previous cases.

"Chief, want me to drive him to the station and you hitch a ride with Rebecca or wait for you?"

"You go ahead. I'll meet you there shortly. Good work, Jacob."

Jacob grabbed the keys mid-air from Kenny's toss.

"Why don't we call him Officer like everyone else who works under you?"

"You've always called him Jacob, so I do to in your presence. After this, I'm sure he'll be strutting around like a peacock, which is much deserved. He caught me up on the details and how the two of you pulled this together. It really was good investigating."

Together, they got into Rebecca's car and pulled out onto the road that led back to Bristol. She dropped him off at the station, with a quick kiss, before returning to the library for the rest of her shift. It had started to snow when she entered, and Jeremy was swamped with patrons. Kids filled the children's section, adults occupied all of the seats, and the check-out line was four deep.

"I'm here. Sorry it took so long." She jumped in, cleared out the line with Jeremy and checked in with the seated patrons. Children left with the adults as they checked out. "That was a little crazy," she admitted.

"They all showed up in the last twenty minutes, so it wasn't crazy for long. What happened?"

With a few adults still seated, they backed up near the office, and Rebecca whispered, "Jacob and I figured out who killed Mr. Josephson. It was perfect. I was working on one thing while he worked on another, and it just came together."

"Congratulations. Am I forgiven now?"

"For what?" she asked.

"For scaring you in the parking lot, and for eating your lunch." He grinned sheepishly.

"For scaring me, yes. For eating my lunch, no. Jilly's is closed now, so I can't get another one."

"I'll pick one up for you the next time I come in, deal?"

She considered the offer with her lips pinched to one side. "Yes, but I'm still going to get you back next year, when you least expect it."

"That's fair." He gathered what few items he must have entered with and left, waving on the way out.

Rebecca spent the rest of the shift cleaning up the disaster left by the children. More patrons came and went, then it was time to go home. Since Kenny wasn't the lead on this investigation, Jacob was left to do the paperwork. The girls came over for dinner with Kenny, followed by dessert.

"Dad said there was a special treat!" Megan bounced on her little seven-year-old toes, having celebrated her birthday last month along with Melanie.

"Yes. The two of you are going to go outside with your father and gather bowls of snow."

"Ummm, snow? Are we making snowballs?" Melanie asked.

"We are having *sugar on snow* for dessert."

Both girls stared at Rebecca. Megan broke the awkward silence. "Why would we do that?"

"Just go get four bowls of clean snow, and I'll show you."

The trio put on their boots and went outside for only a few minutes before returning with the fluffy white powder.

"On my way home, I drove out to Fundamental Elements and picked up some plain donuts." There was no excitement in the responses.

"Plain? Why plain? My favorite is chocolate frosted."

"And mine is sugar jelly."

Both girls were shushed by Kenny. "Let her finish."

"I'm heating some of the maple syrup from Mr. Josephson in a pot on the stove. We're going to drizzle it over the snow to make *sugar on snow*. You eat it, and some of the snow, with the donut to cut how sweet the syrup is, and..." She took a jar of dill pickle spears out of the fridge. "You also eat a dill pickle to add salt. It all balances making the perfect spring snack."

"With this new snow, it doesn't feel much like spring," added Kenny.

"Don't worry much about it. We're expecting warm weather again in the next few days, and mud season will be back in all its glory."

The little family gathered at the kitchen island, Melanie and Megan sitting on stools, Kenny and Rebecca standing. The adults drizzled the warm syrup over the snow which caused it to solidify into something between chewy candy and hard candy. The girls twirled the golden sweetness on their utensils, remembering every so often to take a bite of the donut or pickle.

Rebecca lifted her spoon covered in snow and syrup. "To Mr. Josephson."

Kenny nodded, and the girls cheered, "To Mr. Josephson." Though they weren't in on the reason for her dedication, she was sure Mr. Josephson would have appreciated the recognition.

The night ended with hugs and goodbyes as Kenny took the girls home for bed. They were still in school this week. He walked back to the front door after both were secured in the back of his SUV.

"Congratulations on today, future Mrs. Towne."

"Thanks, Mr. Towne. I'm looking forward to the rest of our sappy lives together."

PLEASE LEAVE A REVIEW!

⭐ ⭐ ⭐ ⭐ ⭐

Virginia K Bennett

An Appetite for Solving Crime

THANK YOU FOR READING MY BOOK!
I WOULD LOVE TO READ YOUR FEEDBACK ON
FACEBOOK, INSTAGRAM, AMAZON, OR
SIMPLY SEND AN EMAIL TO:
authorvirginiakbennett@gmail.com

Recipe

<u>Maple Snickerdoodles</u>
Ingredients:
2 1/2 cups all-purpose flour
2 tsp cornstarch
3/4 tsp baking soda
1/2 tsp salt
1 1/2 tsp ground cinnamon
1/2 tsp cream of tartar
3/4 cup unsalted butter (softened)
2/3 cup light brown sugar
1/3 cup granulated sugar
1/4 cup pure maple syrup
1 large egg
1/2 tsp maple extract
1/4 cup granulated sugar
2 tsp ground cinnamon

Preheat oven to 350 degrees Fahrenheit. Line two baking sheets with parchment paper.

Combine flour, cornstarch, baking soda, salt, cinnamon and cream of tartar in a medium mixing bowl and set aside.

In a stand mixer, beat butter, brown sugar and granulated sugar until light and creamy. Add syrup, egg and maple extract, beating until combined while scraping the sides and bottom as needed. Add the flour mixture and beat until well combined.

In a shallow bowl, combine remaining sugar and cinnamon for coating the dough balls.

Roll dough into approximately 24 balls by hand. Roll each ball in the cinnamon-sugar mixture and place a couple inches apart on the prepared baking sheets. (Do not flatten)

Bake for 11-13 minutes, until the edges are set but the centers are still soft. Allow the cookies to firm up on the baking sheet before transferring to wire racks to cool completely.

Makes approximately 2 dozen cookies.

Also by Virginia K. Bennett

A Newfound Lake Cozy Mystery:

* * *

The Mysteries of Cozy Cove:

Much Ado About Muffin

It's All or Muffin

Muffin to Lose

Nothing Ventured, Muffin Gained

You Ain't Seen Muffin Yet

Here Goes Muffin

About the Author

When she's not writing on her couch with her two cats, Twyla and Geo, Virginia is busy teaching middle school math, grocery shopping, cooking or spending time with her husband and son. Together, her small family loves to go geocaching and visit theme parks.

Mysteries have always been an interesting challenge for Virginia, much like watching a magician perform. Unless you want to hear the entire thought process behind who she thinks is the killer and why, you might want to avoid watching any movies together.

The path to publishing a book is different for everyone and her path is full of twists and turns. Thank you to those who support the journey.

facebook.com/VirginiaKBennett
instagram.com/authorvkbennett

Made in United States
North Haven, CT
14 March 2024